UNA STUBBS'
FAIRY TALES

UNA STUBBS'
FAIRY TALES

ILLUSTRATED
BY
GRAM
CORBETT

WARD LOCK LIMITED·LONDON

First published in Great Britain in 1987
by Ward Lock Limited, 8 Clifford Street,
London W1X 1RB, an Egmont Company.

Text set in Horley Old Style
by Dorchester Typesetting

Printed and bound in Great Britain by
Purnell Book Production Limited

British Library Cataloguing in Publication Data

Stubbs, Una
   Una Stubbs fairy tales.
   I. Title   II. Corbett, Gram
   823′.914[J]   PZ8

ISBN 0-7063-6561-5

CONTENTS

Dear Parents

If you read these stories to your children, please scrape the barrel for your best-acting talents, using as many varied voices and accents as possible. It will make it far more interesting for you and your offspring, and will stop the temptation to skip chunks thinking that they won't notice!

I hope you all enjoy it.

love Una.

CINDER-ELLA

A romantic story full of sadness, humour, drama and magic – not just for girls.

THE CHARACTERS

Benjamin, Ella's father	. . . *soft-spoken, kindly man.*
Antoinette, Ella's mother	. . . *(she has no dialogue).*
Ella (later Cinder-Ella)	. . . *gentle but determined.*
Magenta, Cinder-Ella's stepmother	. . . *shrill, pretentious and as common as muck.*
Plum, Cinder-Ella's stepsister	. . . *like her Mum, only younger.*
Purple, Cinder-Ella's stepsister	. . . *like her Mum, only younger.*
King's Messenger	. . . *as near to Bob Hoskins as you can get him.*
Fairy Godmother	. . . *down-to-earth, no-nonsense and quite mumsy.*
Prince Patrick	. . . *strong, romantic but not soppy.*
Mice	. . . *high pitched, only don't hurt yourself.*
Miscellaneous noises	. . . *giggles, slurps, burps, heartbeats, and various grunts and sighs.*

"Once upon a time," – it's funny how lots of stories start like this, isn't it? – well anyway, years and years ago, long before you or I or Auntie or Uncle or even the Queen Mother was born, a man called Benjamin and his wife Antoinette lived very happily with their dear little daughter Ella in a large house on top of a steep, green hill.

Although it was quite a large house, it was very cosy, full of pretty furniture and bits and bobs, and it smelt of flowers, furniture polish, clean towels and toast. Benjamin, Antoinette and Ella loved their house almost as much as they loved each other.

At the end of each day all three of them, with big mugs of hot chocolate, would plonk down in the largest chair (they called it the 'cuddling chair') and tell each other funny stories. The gigglings, slurpings and kissings goodnight could be heard by the people living in the houses at the bottom of the hill. They would all start giggling too saying, "Just hark at those three up there. What a lovely racket."

Then something terrible happened. Ella's sweet, gentle mother became very ill, and although her father chased everywhere for the very best doctors, none of them could find the right medicine to make her well again, so very sadly she died. Ella and Benjamin spent many days crying softly together, and all the people at the bottom of the hill cried softly too. Antoinette had been such a lovely person that everyone missed her very much.

Over the next few years Ella and her father worked very hard to make each other happy. They kept the house and garden just the way it had always been. They even told each other funny stories in the cuddling chair, but despite all this, Ella could see that her father was lonely for a wife.

One day, while they were drinking hot chocolate, Benjamin told

Ella that he had met a lady at work who was lonely too because her husband had run away. So, he explained, they were going to be married and she would come and live with them with her two daughters.

"Oh Ella," he said in his usual tender voice, "we will be a proper family again." Ella was so pleased for her father, it made her very happy that he would have a wife and that she would have two ready-made sisters to play with and share their lovely home.

On the day when Benjamin had gone to collect everyone, Ella leapt out of bed. She gave the furniture an extra polish, put fresh flowers all over the house, laid a delicious tea in front of the fire and lit candles everywhere to welcome them. She was so excited that her tummy kept making loud rumbling noises and she very nearly didn't hear the carriage rattling up the hill. She ran downstairs, threw open the door, and there standing *on* the flower-beds were her new family.

They must have been very excited too, because they all barged into the house, crashing Ella against the wall and quite forgetting to wipe their muddy shoes.

"BENJAMIN," shouted Ella's new stepmother (she had a very loud voice), "LET'S GET THE INTRODUCTIONS OVER WITH SHARPISH."

"Oh, yes dear, of course," he said softly, trying not to blush. (Ella always wanted to cuddle him when he blushed). "Now where shall I start," he said. "Um . . . er . . . Ella my darling . . . um . . . this . . . um . . ."

Ella had never seen her father so nervous before, he was usually so quietly confident.

"OH GET ON WITH IT BENJ' FOR GAWD'S SAKE," said Ella's stepmother even louder than ever. "OH I'LL DO IT, I'M YOUR NEW STEPMOTHER MY NAME IS MAGENTA

SOME PEOPLE CALL ME MAG' BUT YOU MUST CALL ME MOTHER THESE ARE YOUR NEW SISTERS DON'T PICK YOUR NOSES ANGELS THIS IS PLUM THIS IS PURPLE AND I SUPPOSE YOU MUST BE ELLA THAT'S A QUEER NAME FUNNY LOOKING SCRAP AIN'T SHE BENJ' NOT LIKE MY TWO BEAUTIES WHERE'S TEA I'M PARCHED."

She said this all in one breath, her voice getting shriller and shriller, and had it got any more shrill, only dogs would have heard her. But Ella thought that she was quite right – her two daughters were very beautiful.

Her new mother was a fine-looking woman, with huge bosoms and bits of them showing over the top of her dress, which was a dark purply colour made of stiff material that crackled and sparked when she moved. Her hair was in a thick, curly bundle on top of her head and dyed to match her frock; her lips and nails were painted the same.

Plum looked just like her mother but younger and shorter. Her sister Purple must have looked like her runaway father as she was very tall and slim and chilly looking with a nose to match her name and her frock.

It was difficult for Ella not to notice these things. She always tried not to have unkind thoughts, it was just that her new family seemed . . . um . . . unusual. "But", she thought, pushing her small, round glasses back up her nose, "I'm sure we'll all get on very happily together."

"Now my dears let's have some tea," said Ella's father pointing the way. Plum and Purple must have been ravenous because they ran and jumped across the furniture in their muddy shoes, knocking over candles and pots of flowers to get there first, and Magenta must have been just too tired to correct them.

When they saw the tea Ella had taken such care to make, they cried, "'Snot much to eat, is there Mum?"

"WELL GET STUCK IN QUICK POPPETS, ELSE ELLA WILL GET MORE THAN YOU."

They needn't have worried. Ella was far too excited to eat. She just sat with them at the table, her eyes getting larger and larger with disbelief.

Her stepmother grabbed a pile of cakes and scones for herself and left the table with them to sit in front of the fire, in the best chair, the cuddling chair, which was almost too small for her, and it creaked angrily.

Plum and Purple scrambled and fought for the biggest cakes. The ones they didn't like the look of they threw into the air, or at each other. The ones they did like, they rammed into their mouths as fast as they could, drinking tea and screaming and shouting at each other, all at the same time. When they had had sufficient, they slumped back in their chairs, put their feet on the table and let out two long burps, without saying pardon or putting their hands over their sticky mouths.

Ella's father was stunned with shock too and his eyes were as round as Ella's glasses. It had all happened so quickly.

After a long pause Magenta let out an even louder burp, and when she turned round, smiling sweetly at her daughters, she had even more jam and crumbs round her mouth than they did. Ella and her father, who always saw the funny side of everything, almost giggled until she squawked out: "NOW MY TWO LITTLE ANGELS, BEDDY-BYES. LOOK OVER THE HOUSE AND CHOOSE THE BEST ROOMS FOR YOURSELVES. ELLA, YOU CLEAR AWAY THE TEA THINGS, THEN CLEAR AWAY YOURSELF."

Ella was quite pleased to have some time to herself. She quietly washed the dishes, and when they were all sparkling back on the shelves, she slowly closed the door and tip-toed upstairs to the comfort of her cosy room – except it was no longer cosy! Plum and Purple had stripped it of almost everything – her toys, dolls, her books and pictures – all that was left was her bed and chest of drawers. Ella didn't want to worry her father any more, so she crawled into her bed and tried to sleep, which was very difficult as her sisters kept screaming to each other across the landing.

"PLU-U-U-M, DO YOU FINK YOU'LL LIKE IT HERE?"

"I DUNNO PURPLE. SPECKY FOUR EYES LOOKS A SOPPY DRIP, SO DOES HER DAD."

Then it was Magenta's turn, "OH BENJ', I THOUGHT YOU WOULD HAVE A MUCH NICER HOUSE THAN THIS."

Ella pulled the sheets tightly over her ears. "My poor darling daddy," she thought, trying not to let the tears run out of her eyes. "You must have been so lonely to let this happen . . . or perhaps everyone is just over-excited. It will be better tomorrow, I know it will."

But sad to say, each day got worse than the one before. Plum and Purple behaved like farmyard animals, wrecking the house at the speed of lightning, Magenta's temper became more unpleasant by the minute, and their pretty faces became uglier and uglier. Poor Benjamin looked a sad and broken man, who blamed himself for the tragic mistake he had made. Eventually, he became so pale and thin that he was too weak to eat the food Ella tried to feed him. He just took to his bed and died of a broken heart, which happened to a lot of people in those days.

Poor Ella thought she would never smile again, for not only had she lost her beloved father, but her dearest friend in all the world, and she pressed her face into the pillow which was already wet with tears. Plum and Purple seized this opportunity to treat Ella even more cruelly than before.

"STOP BLUBBERING MOPEY-DOPEY," they screamed, kicking open the door, and waving their bedtime candles (as electric light had not yet been invented). "WE'VE COME TO CHEER YOU UP WITH A CONCERT."

The two monsters began an absurd show consisting of rude signs and silly faces. Before Ella could stop them Plum's candle was knocked on to the bed, setting it ablaze.

The two stupid Steps stood starched still with shock, but Ella grabbed all her clothes from the chest of drawers, using them to smother the flames.

When at last the fire was out, all that was left was one small, damp pillow lying in the middle of the room. The dress Ella was wearing and her little face and body were as black as soot, which delighted her wicked steps.

"CINDER-CINDER-BURNT-TO-A-CINDER," they chanted. "WE SHALL CALL YOU CINDERS. CINDERS-SCRUB-THE-FLOORS-CINDERS-CHOP-THE-WOOD-CINDERS-LIGHT-THE-FIRES."

But their bad behaviour only made Cinder-Ella determined they would not break her spirit as they had her father's. So in the evening, when her work was done and the others were snoring loudly, she crouched by the stove in the kitchen (sharing a dry crust of bread with the kitchen mice) and gave herself a strict talking to.

"As soon as it starts getting light I shall run down the hill to tell someone about my wicked Steps' cruelty."

"Of course you must," squeaked six little voices. "Nobody should be ill-treated, not even mice. Hurry, hurry, it's getting light.

They pushed her through the door, squeaking "Good luck Cinder-Ella", though not too loudly for fear of disturbing the snorers upstairs.

Ella ran and ran, the wet grass washing her feet. "I expect this is what Heaven is like," she thought, and she smiled the smile she thought she would never use again. Suddenly, through the mist came the eerie shape of a stranger on horseback. Cinders picked up a sharp rock and hid behind a tree.

"Miss, Miss," the stranger called. "Don't be scared."

"KEEP YOUR DISTANCE," roared little Cinders, trying to sound fierce.

"I understand, Missy, so you stay there and I'll stay here while you listen to what I have to say. It's very important." He cleared his throat loudly first. "I am the King's personal messenger. Now the Prince, that's the King's son Missy, is having a huge twenty-first birthday party at the palace tonight and he wants everyone to share it with him. I am delivering all the invitations. It's taken me two whole months mind, and these are the last ones I am glad to say."

"Who are they for?" Cinder-Ella asked, still brandishing the sharp rock.

"Why the four ladies what live on top of this hill. You are one of them, aren't you Missy?"

"Yes, but I wouldn't be invited."

"Didn't I say everyone," he laughed. "I'll let you into a secret, what no-one else knows about. 'The-Prince-is-looking-for-a-wife',", and he tapped his nose, winked one eye, handed her the four invitations and galloped off through the mist.

Cinders' tummy rumbled with excitement as she raced back home, just in time to make everyone's breakfast.

"YOU'RE LATE," spat Magenta.

"I'm sorry," smiled Cinders, and she handed out the invitations to her stepmother and sisters. On reading them, they started throwing boiled eggs at each other, screaming hysterically.

"CINDERS, WE HAVE BEEN INVITED TO A PARTY AT THE PALACE."

"Yes, I know," she replied. "So have I."

"WHAAATTT," and they snatched away her invitation and threw it on the stove.

"NOW YOU HAVEN'T," they shrieked. "BESIDES YOU HAVE NOTHING TO WEAR. YOU HAD AN ACCIDENT WITH A FIRE, REMEMBER?"

Cinder-Ella trembled as they swept out of the room chanting "SHALL WE WEAR OUR LAVENDER OR FUCHSIA OR LILAC OR HYACINTH OR DAMSON OR . . ."

Cinder-Ella put her fingers in her ears. It was too much for her to bear. Soon she had to collect the dresses they had chosen, to launder and press.

On the stroke of seven, the three Steps gathered in the hall to show off their finery. Oh crumbs! What a sight they looked, it was hard for Cinders not to giggle. As they scrambled into the carriage, she could see that the back of their dresses were all hitched up in their knickers, where they hadn't checked after visiting the loo. Now, you and I would probably have let them go off like that as a punishment, but Cinders was much kinder than us and called after them pointing to their mistake.

Once they had gone, Cinder-Ella curled up by the stove with her mice friends and they all had a good sob at the unfairness of life. Every person in the land would be at the party, except Cinder-Ella; they all closed their eyes and gave a jerky sigh.

"Oh what a sigh," said a voice that sounded like a glass bell.

Standing in a shaft of light was the most beautiful creature they had ever seen. Her dress and hair was like a swirling white mist, dotted here and there with twinkling drops of dew. Her shoes were made of carved ice which left frosty footprints on the kitchen floor, and she carried a long needle-thin icicle with a real star from the sky on top. She was brilliant.

"Are you a ghosty?" asked the mice hiding behind Cinder-Ella.

"Sometimes I wish I was. No, of course I'm not. I'm Cinders' Fairy Godmother. Now, what's all this nonsense about you lot not going to the party," she chimed.

They opened their mouths to tell her, but she pealed, "It's a load of rubbish, of course you can go. Fetch me that big fat saucepan and put it down here. Now watch this – this is really good."

She rattled the star and said "CHING" and turned the saucepan into a glass carriage. Everyone gasped and applauded.

"Oh, that's not the best bit, watch this one," she said. "Mice, I hope you are feeling strong tonight. CHING." And she turned them into six tiny white ponies to pull the carriage. They were so proud they couldn't stop grinning.

"Now Cinder-Ella, it's your turn. What would you like to wear?"

"Please may I have shoes and a dress like yours?"

"Oh, do you like it? It's new. Yes of course you can, only I'll make it of stronger stuff then mine. CHING. Oh, Cinder-Ella, that's the best I've ever done, you look a picture. I even managed to get diamonds round your glasses," and she helped Ella into the carriage.

"Now here comes the boring bit. I'm letting you go to this party, as long as you are sensible while you're there and get back no later than twelve o'clock midnight. If you don't, I shall have to punish you, and I wouldn't let you stay out so late again as I couldn't trust you. Promise?"

"I promise. How can I thank you enough?"

"By carrying on being such a good girl," answered her godmother, and she gave Cinders a kiss on both cheeks making them glisten even more.

"I suddenly feel nervous, I've never been to a party before," whispered Cinder-Ella.

"More rubbish. It's a piece of cake. If you can't think of anything to say, then listen till you can. If you don't know which spoons to start with, wait to see which one the Prince uses first. And if that excited tummy of yours starts rumbling, simply say, 'Oh listen to that thunder.' Have you got a clean hanky? Be sensible, and remember your promise, no later than twelve. CHING." And with that Cinders' carriage went off into the night, speeding towards the palace.

Cinder-Ella could hear the music and laughter as she walked up the palace steps. The large doors opened and she stepped inside. Suddenly the music and laughter stopped. A voice behind her whispered, "I was afraid you wasn't coming, Missy, you look a proper smasher." It was the King's kind messenger. "Let me introduce you to the Prince."

He took her arm and steered her through the crowd, who gasped at Cinders' fresh beauty. "Who is she?" they mouthed, craning their necks like giraffes to see more of her.

"Your Highness, I want you to meet a little friend of mine," the messenger boasted, only because he was so proud to know this lovable treasure.

The Prince smiled and said, "Hullo, I'm Prince Patrick."

Cinders curtsied like a daisy, replying, "Hullo, I'm very pleased to meet you."

The Prince took her hand and asked her if she liked dancing.

She said she did and away they whirled into the middle of the room, with everyone nodding and smiling knowingly. Even her stepfamily stood there with stiff grins, hissing through clenched teeth, "If he's going to dance with that scrag-end all night, it's not going to be much of a party. I bet Cinder-Ella is having more fun at home doing our washing."

The Prince did dance with Cinders all night, chattering and giggling, whirling and dancing, quite forgetting all about the time. TIME!! Cinder-Ella came to a grinding halt.

"Prince, what time do you make it?" she asked breathlessly.

"Five minutes to twelve. Why?"

"Because I promised my, my . . . mother I'd be in by twelve. Thank you for the *best* evening, lovely to meet you, I must fly," and she darted through the crowd kicking off her glass shoes so that she could run faster.

Cinder-Ella dived into her carriage, her heart beating out the seconds – nine-ten-eleven – "Oh quickly, quickly, please", she called.

As they came to the top of the steep, green hill, suddenly her carriage and white dress had disappeared and Cinder-Ella ran into the house dressed in her old rags.

Her godmother was waiting for her, tapping her icy shoes. "What time do you call this?" she chimed at Cinders.

Cinder-Ella looked crestfallen and whispered, "Sorry."

"Sorry isn't good enough. I was worried sick, anything could have happened to you. Now just sit there and think about it. I'll see you again when I'm not so cross," and she was gone.

Cinders didn't have time to think for long because Magenta, Plum and Purple came screeching home, laughing and shouting that it was the most *"WUNDERFUL PARTY AND THE PRINCE WOULD ONLY DANCE WITH US ALL NIGHT*

AND HE SAID HE WOULD CALL LATER TO TELL US WHICH ONE HE HAD DECIDED TO MARRY." Then their pretend smiles dropped and they all stomped off to bed.

Back at the palace the Prince picked up the glass shoes, which were still warm, and clutched them to his chest, saying sadly to the messenger, "I didn't even ask her name, I'll never see her again."

But the messenger answered, "You just leave it to me, Your Highness. Tomorrow we'll go for a little gallop, somewhere interesting."

After a sleepless night, sad Cinder-Ella was back at her chores, day-dreaming about Prince Patrick's kind face and the lovely time they had spent together.

"CINDERS," came a squawk from upstairs, "THE PRINCE AND HIS COMMON MESSENGER ARE GALLOPING UP THE HILL: HE'S COMING TO TELL US WHICH ONE OF US HE WANTS, SO YOU KEEP OUT OF THE WAY OR THE SIGHT OF YOU WILL MAKE THE PRINCE THROW UP."

Her three Steps crashed downstairs and opened the door, shouting "YOO-HOO PRINCEY, HERE WE ARE. COME IN AND HAVE A CUP OF TEA, BUT LEAVE YOUR COMMON MESSENGER OUTSIDE."

The two men nudged each other, looking incredulously at this clutter of noisy females who were trying to curtsey with legs that refused to bend. They ended up like a pile of worms squirming at the Prince's feet.

"Get up worms, I mean ladies," said the messenger, trying not to laugh. "The Prince is here on an important mission to find the little Missy who dropped these here glass shoes."

"I DID," gushed Magenta, Plum and Purple in unison, clawing for the shoes, ramming their knobbly toes into them in the effort to make them fit.

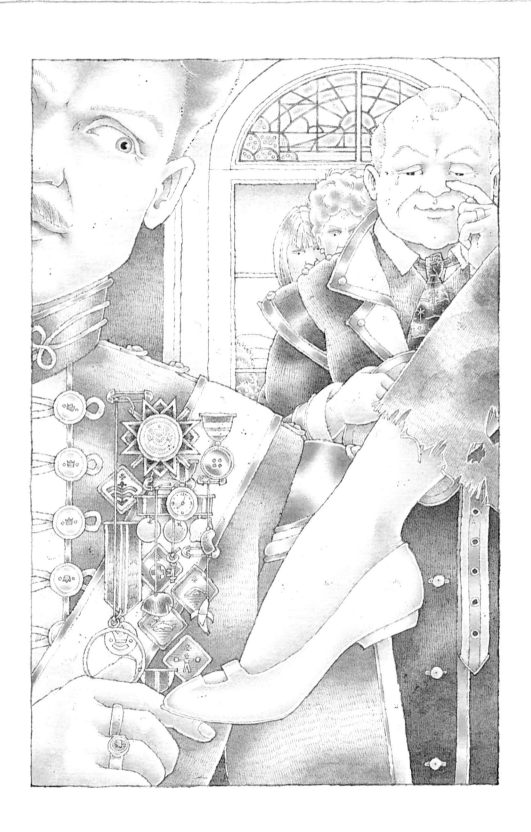

The messenger rescued the shoes quickly before they got broken, saying, "Where is the little Missy who lives here with you?"

"WHAT LITTLE MISSY? ONLY US THREE LADIES LIVE HERE WITH OUR MANGY MAID CALLED CINDER-ELLA."

This unkind remark infuriated the Prince who shouted, "FETCH CINDER-ELLA NOW."

Magenta, Plum and Purple's mouths flopped open and they backed out of the room again, still curtseying, and returned a few seconds later dragging Cinders with them.

The Prince and Cinder-Ella stood gazing at each other for what seemed like ten minutes.

"You left these," said the Prince gently and he handed her the glass shoes.

"Thank you, Your Highness," whispered Cinder-Ella, slipping them on her tiny feet.

Her stepmother's and sisters' faces turned slime green. They staggered from the room and fainted in a heap just outside the door.

"Cinder-Ella", said the Prince, not caring that his messenger was watching, "will you marry me?", and he blushed to the roots of his magnificent red hair, just like her father used to do. So she reached up and gave him a cuddle and whispered "Yes" in his ear. She wanted to kiss him too, but first she ran to hug her dear messenger friend, who was weeping, winking and tapping his nose all at the same time.

So Cinder-Ella left the house on the hill, to marry her Prince at the palace, and their love and happiness brought joy to everyone.

Once a week, whilst Prince Patrick was working, Cinder-Ella would invite her Fairy Godmother for an ice-cream tea and a good gossip. It was during one of these afternoons that Cinder-Ella confessed she had only one worry in the world and that was the welfare of her stepfamily. She pleaded with her godmother to help.

"Oh Cinders, that's a really big job you're asking me to do," said her Fairy Godmother after a long think. "I'm getting a bit long in the tooth. I don't know if I have the power left for something so difficult. I think they are past repair." She looked at her god-daughter's sweet, beseeching face and said, in a flurry of snowflakes, "You're on, it will be my last big challenge before retirement," and then she was gone.

Two months later, Cinder-Ella received an invitation to tea at the house on the hill. As her carriage neared her old home she could see her three Steps running to welcome her; and as they led her happily through the front door, the smell that greeted her was flowers, furniture polish, clean towels and toast.

Cinder-Ella's happiness was complete. Her Fairy Godmother could retire with pride; she had done a magnificent job on her stepfamily, who now spent every waking hour doing good for others. Her father would have been so proud, as indeed was everybody else.

THE TALE OF THE TOWN
AND
COUNTRY MOUSE

A nice short one.

THE CHARACTERS

Country mouse . . . *rural, but certainly not a bumpkin.*

Town mouse . . . *quite posh, but certainly not unpleasant.*

Miscellaneous noises . . . *bird whistles, steamer hooters, car horns, shrill human voices and laughs, cat wailing, and a final sigh.*

In a snug, downy hole, overlooking a stream on the edge of a cornfield, there lived a country mouse.

On waking early one morning, just when the birds were trilling the last few bars of their dawn concert, the country mouse filled his lungs with some fresh air and gazed dreamily at the wonders about him. Dew drops jingling on the cobwebs, the stream trickling in its own time with no particular place to go, and the corn playing with the warm breeze. He felt he would like to share these joys with an old school-friend who had chosen to live in the town. So an invitation was sent and duly accepted.

Although the country mouse's habits were plain and rustic, he emptied his larder of its winter hoard to prepare a welcoming feast for his towny friend. Quantity made up for the lack of fancy ingredients. There was acorn soup, great bowls of mixed leaf salad, cheese flakes, and blackberry beer.

Sadly, the town mouse, who was used to more elegant lunches, just picked at his food. He looked around him, yawning, and said "How can you bear to live stuck out here? It's *dead*, there's nothing to do – it's so *booooooooring*!"

The country mouse couldn't think how a place that had wind-surfing in the spring, barn dances in the summer, barbeques in the winter, and bird concerts all the year round, could possibly be 'booooooooring'. But he was open-minded and always ready to try to understand another animal's way of life, so he agreed to journey back with his friend to have supper and spend the weekend in town, which his friend seemed fidgety to get back to.

As his friend's shoes looked rather flimsy, the country mouse kindly suggested they take his raft. They travelled upstream waving to neighbours, who were enjoying leaf-regattas, mixed bathing and community washing at the water's edge. The neighbours shouted

back friendly words as the two mice floated past.

"Did you know all those creatures?" asked a baffled town mouse.

"Not all of them," replied his friend.

"Well they all said, 'HELLO, NICE DAY' . . . how frightful!"

Frightful is exactly the word the country mouse would have used to describe the next lap of the journey. As the little stream entered the vast river, the minute raft was flung against the river bank, almost capsizing. Giant iron monsters steamed past belching out clouds and carrying humans, but they didn't seem to mind.

It was almost midnight when the tiny tug floated into the city centre. "Not far to go", squeaked the towny, who now seemed to be in his element. He helped the brave little 'captain' up the steps and steered him across a hard, shiny piece of land, which had noisy hooting things racing across it in opposite directions.

"I prefer the tractors we have at home", thought the country mouse as they darted between the angry wheels. "Look at all these things chasing about and not one of *them* knows how to plough – but they look smart enough twinkling in the town's curious red . . . no amber . . . no green moonlight!"

"Home at last," shouted his friend proudly, ending his chum's confused thoughts. "Welcome", he said as he showed the country mouse into a sumptuous place. It had silky walls, a soft woolly floor, a giant dewy cobweb twinkling from the ceiling, and a giant table laden with a half-eaten meal.

"Perfect – champagne, melba toast, Brie, and pecan pie; please *doooo* start!"

The country mouse watched in awe as his sophisticated friend ate so neatly with his mouth shut, looking quite at home in his posh surroundings. "How I wish I wasn't wearing my wellingtons; but, oh, is this food good?!" he thought, whilst also trying to think of something witty to say. He was saved by a bell as twenty humans crashed, laughing, into the room.

The two mice dived behind a silk hanging and watched as one human pressed a button on a big box – a noise came out like a hundred cows kicking over milk buckets. Then the humans all started jumping up and down, shouting "OUCH – OOPS – SORRY DAHLING – HOORAY – YA" and "Isn't this BRILL", over and over.

The town mouse loved it all, clapping his paws and whistling through his teeth, until finally, worn out from the day's adventure, the two mice left the din to catch up on some sleep.

But that was wishful thinking, for the din carried on for hours longer. When it eventually ended, it was replaced by sirens and hootings and the caterwaulings of cats . . . CATS!

"Listen my friend," said a trembling country mouse during a lull, "I feel as fidgety here as you did in my home. I must leave before my head explodes. I have to live at a more peaceful pace than you."

So the two friends shook paws and agreed that it takes all sorts of mice to make a world. How lucky that mice are not all made the same, or it would be a very dull world indeed . . . which it certainly is not.

JACK AND THE BEANSTALK

A story of sadness, humour, terror, bravery, love and magic, and of good conquering evil.

THE CHARACTERS

Jack	. . .	*as croaky as possible without choking.*
Lucy, Jack's mother	. . .	*gentle, but not too wet.*
Butcher	. . .	*like a grumpy Bob Hoskins.*
Grey fairy	. . .	*matter-of-fact, but world-weary.*
Daphne	. . .	*almost too delicate for words.*
Giant	. . .	*gruff, loud and slobbery.*
Miscellaneous noises	. . .	*moos, mews, bellows, tuts, yelps, grunts and burps.*

In a very modest cottage, deep in the country there lived a kind, lonely widow called Lucy with her son Jack and one cow called Margaret.

Lucy had the sort of kindness that bordered on foolishness. She almost ruined her son with too much love and devotion because of her concern that Jack had no father.

If, for instance, Margaret was a bit short on milk, Lucy didn't complain as long as her darling Jack had enough nourishment. Lucy was far too soft to discipline Margaret, even though she was a lazy cow who preferred fluttering her eyelashes at the bull in the field next door, to eating buttercups and grass to produce creamy milk for butter, yoghurt and cheese. Lucy would sometimes go for days without eating, but stupidly she couldn't understand why she felt wobbly and unable to get the work done.

Sadly, as Jack grew older, he began to take advantage of his mother's softness. Jack was a kind boy in many ways, who truly loved his mother, but he just didn't think. When he was asked to clean his boots, he would cover his face and hands with polish, tie the duster round his head like a turban, and saunter through the village saying he was an Indian prince. Milking time was no better. He treated Margeret like an adored puppy, romping with her and chasing her until her milk turned all curdly. His poor mother found in the end it was quicker to do everything herself.

At school, Jack didn't pay attention to his studies, but he worked very hard instead at being the classroom clown. He preferred the laughter of his friends to any success with lessons. Lucy pleaded with her son to take his schooling seriously. She warned him that when he left school there would be no job for someone who could only pull funny faces.

Sure enough, when Jack grew up, although everybody thought

he was very amusing, no-one wanted to give him work as they knew he was too lazy. Yet Lucy still continued to spoil her son, allowing him to take money from their savings tin for noisy evenings out with his chums . . . until one day their savings were all gone.

"Oh Jack," his foolish mother wept, "we are penniless, and all because I've been too soft with you. Unless we are to starve to death, we must both turn over a new leaf, starting from now." Poor Lucy trembled with her unfamiliar sternness. There was nothing left to do, she cried, but to sell poor old Margaret. She told Jack not to come home until he had got a good price for the cow at the local butchers.

Poor Margaret couldn't believe her fate. As Jack led her into the village, she kept twisting her neck, moo-ing her last good-byes to her boy-friend. The bull beat the fence with his horns in protest and bellowed with sadness as Jack and Margaret disappeared down the lane to the butchers.

"What do you call this, a bonebag?" muttered the toothy butcher, prodding the now sobbing Margaret. Jack quickly covered the poor cow's ears. "You should have kept her well fed if you wanted her to fetch a good price," and, rattling his teeth in disgust, he opened the till and tossed Jack nothing more than a bag of beans. "That's all she's worth, now SHOOO", he said, almost spitting out his dentures onto the counter.

Silly Jack, who had no idea about finance, looked at the bag of brightly-coloured beans and thought he had a bargain. He gave Margaret a last loving pat, and then raced off home to tell his mother of their good fortune.

"MUM – MUM," Jack shouted, speeding up the path. Jack's mother, meanwhile, had been planning that they would buy a chicken and a goat, and perhaps even a warm jumper for Jack. On hearing her son's boyish call, she eagerly hurried to meet him.

Jack led his mother into the kitchen, stood in front of her, panting, and proudly handed over the bag of beans. Poor Lucy opened the bag. On seeing the contents, she sank onto a chair and stared at her son in disbelief.

She did not speak for a very long time. Then, quietly, she said, "Jack-I-don't-know-what-to-say-to-you-I-feel-as-if-you-have-taken-away-my-last-breath." She got up and flung the beans into the garden. Then she turned to Jack and, to his surprise, shouted, "NOW GO UPSTAIRS AND DON'T COME DOWN TILL MORNING." Jack's mother wandered round and round the kitchen, weeping and wringing her hands, not knowing how they were going to survive.

In the morning, Jack was woken by a sinking feeling inside him, but as it was still dark, he closed his eyes and tried to sleep some more. But sleep wouldn't come. He stared at the ceiling, waiting for it to get light. He waited and waited, but two hours later it was still dark. Jack began to feel hungry and soon the gurglings inside his tummy became almost deafening. He could hear his mother working downstairs and couldn't understand this, so he got out of bed and felt his way in the darkness to the window. What a shock he got. There, outside his window, blocking out the daylight, was the biggest tree he had ever seen. It was so tall that Jack couldn't see where it ended.

"MUM – MUM," Jack shrieked, "CAN I COME DOWN YET?" I HAVE TO SHOW YOU WHAT'S GROWN IN THE GARDEN." Before she could reply, he was downstairs dragging her outside with him.

Jack and his mother clutched each other in case what they were seeing was a dream, or even a nightmare. Nowhere in the world could there be a tree as whopping as this one, not even in America.

Its trunk twisted and coiled like a giant multi-coloured rope; its branches reached so high that they disappeared through the clouds; and all the way up it was hung with juicy, green beans and red flowers. It was a brilliant, if not bewildering, sight. It was a great, giant, beanstalk.

If Jack couldn't do much else he could climb trees, and before he could be stopped he was shinning up the beanstalk with ease. His mother tried unsuccessfully to grab his fast-disappearing ankles.

After a few minutes Jack peered down through the branches to see his mother, looking like a tiny ant, waving and pleading to him from the ground below. Jack wanted to wave back to the tiny speck, but he needed both arms to hold onto the beanstalk. He continued on his long journey upwards – it was as if he was being drawn by some great force outside his own feckless mind.

At last, Jack could see the top of the great tree leading through a vast hole in the sky. He pulled himself through the hole and flopped, tired and panting, to the ground. Slowly opening his eyes, Jack looked around him. This, he decided, was the ugliest place in the Universe. There were no trees, grass or flowers, or any sign of anything living. All he could see were grey, stone castles dotted all over a dusty grey landscape. An icy wind blew the dust in whistling, whirling, ghostly shapes which seemed furious at Jack's presence. They beat against him, buffeting and prodding him. Then they lifted him right off the ground and blew him towards the vast hole. Jack had to cling to the branches of the beanstalk with all his might. Then, just when his strength was leaving him, Jack felt his body being wound round and round in a cocoon of warm, grey silk and he was lowered slowly to the ground again. The grey cloth slipped from his shoulders and flapped angrily in front of him. "Oh, leave off wind, for goodness sake," came a breathless voice from the folds of the silk, and, unbelievably, the wind obeyed. There, in front of Jack stood an old, sweet-faced lady. Her billowing dress and hair was of the softest grey, and she carried a tall wand with a silver peacock on top.

"Whatever brought you to this dump?" the grey lady asked Jack, who was bowing and nodding at her like a chicken. So Jack rattled off his story.

When he had finished, she smiled. "Terrific! That's just as I planned it," she said. "Do you remember your dear father, Jack?"

Jack stared cautiously at the lady for a moment, and then he whispered "No, I don't. When I once asked my mother about him, she wept so much that I couldn't bear to mention his name again."

"Listen to me," the woman said kindly, "and I will tell you a story – and the reason why your mother could never speak of your father. But before I do, you must promise to obey me in every way, for I am a fairy and far tougher than your mother."

Jack stared at his dusty boots, feeling quite guilty and ashamed of his past silly behaviour, and he promised the fairy that she could really trust him. So the fairy began.

"Your father was a wealthy man who worked very hard, not only for you and your mother, but for the whole town. Anyone who was in trouble came to him for help, and no one was ever turned away. He even sought out those who were too meek to ask. Because of this, he was a much-loved and respected man.

"In a neighbouring village there lived a giant who was jealous of your father's hard-earned wealth and popularity and he set out to destroy your father. Early one morning, he boomed for his dithery wife and told her they were 'going a-visiting'. Now, as I said Jack, your father never turned anyone away, and even though he had heard of the giant's evil behaviour, he invited him inside. The giant pretended to cry and, sobbing, urged your father to look out to sea through a pair of binoculars he was carrying. There was a fleet of ships caught in a tidal wave, and many sailors were being flung overboard.

"Your father was moved by the giant's new turn of heart. When he saw that what the blubbering ogre had told him was true, he summoned all his servants to prepare his largest ship. With your father at the helm, the brave crew set sail to help."

At this, Jack's eyes misted over with pride and his mouth plopped open. The fairy tapped it shut again, put an arm round his shoulders, and continued. . .

"The evil giant had escorted your father to the beach. He waited until the ship was on the horizon, then he huffed and puffed as hard as he could. This caused the sea to be even more violent than the tidal wave he had made earlier that morning. Your father's ship had no chance and sank like a pebble.

"The evil giant thumped back to your home, and he rampaged through it, ordering his wife to steal everything of value. As soon as the house was empty, he dragged your mother from it, with you in her arms, and burnt your home to the ground. He then tried to snatch you from your mother, Jack, but she fell to her knees and pleaded so piteously that the giant agreed to set you both free – on one condition. Your mother must never, ever, tell a single soul about what had happened or you would both be destroyed too.

"Your poor mother travelled for days to find a modest home and, with a broken heart, brought up her fatherless son in poverty. Meanwhile, the evil giant was living in the comfort that was rightfully yours – and all because of your father's kindness."

On finishing the story, the fairy fluttered silently round Jack giving him time to digest it all.

"Now, Jack," she said, landing breathlessly in front of him, "you may wonder why on earth I didn't help your father . . . well . . . sometimes . . . when fairies get to my age their magic starts to disappear, and that's what happened to me. I am sorry to say I was powerless to help. However, I've rested up over the years. I've been watching over you and your mum, Jack, and, to tell you the truth, I wasn't best pleased with how you were turning out. So I started practising again, gently at first, with the butcher and beans bit. I was tickled pink with the beanstalk and how I got you to climb it, but I can't afford to be big-headed. I know I haven't got long before my powers leave me forever. So, Jack, there is no time for your larking about – this is serious stuff. You *must* find the giant and get back all that belongs to you, or you and your mother will die of hunger. He lives in castle number 49."

With a tired jump, and much heavy breathing and creaking of knees, the fairy fluttered jerkily into a grey wisp and was gone.

"What a day I've had," muttered Jack, "but what a life my poor Mother has suffered, and I was no help. I will do everything I can to make my poor Mum happy and comfortable in her old age. You'll see, fairy," he called into the distance, "I won't let you down." And, remembering that time was short, he ran bravely towards the eerie castles in search of number 49.

"46 . . . 47 . . . 48 . . . not long now", panted the weak and starving Jack. Before much longer, Jack was standing nervously in front of the huge door of castle number 49. "Ugh, it's the biggest and most spooky-looking castle I've ever seen." Only someone with no heart could live in such a bleak and ugly place, he thought. How on earth, he wondered, was he going to reach the rusty knocker on a door that was covered in bubbling green slime. He gulped twice and leapt at it, rattling it as hard as he could before slithering to the ground. He listened for movement inside. He could hear scurrying footsteps, but they faded away, so he repeated his task again. This time the scurrying became louder, and Jack could hear the door being unbolted. He counted ten bolts in all! Jack scrambled to his feet and recited a quick ditty to make himself feel better:

"He may be big and I am small,
But he's only a person after all.
He cleans his teeth like you and me,
And even does a giant pee."

Jack clenched and unclenched his hands, ground his teeth together, and took long, deep breaths in an effort to control his fear, while he waited for the menacing door to open and reveal . . . oh gulp . . . oh phew! . . . not the giant as Jack had dreaded, but a tiny, wretched woman. Jack had never seen someone look so thin and exhausted. Even his own poor mum would have looked quite roly-poly beside her. It was difficult to tell if she was aged thirty or ninety. She was such a sad wreck, trembling and twitching so much, that Jack felt brave enough to beg for a bed for the night and a crust of bread. The poor woman flapped her bony hands to shoo the boy away, but Jack stood his ground. The old crock made little mewing sounds, glancing nervously up and down the street. Then grabbing Jack's sleeve, she pulled him inside and heaved the enormous door shut.

The woman dragged Jack along a long echoing hallway, past a small cage with three staring prisoners jammed inside. He shuddered as he was led through room after dingy room, until they reached a vast kitchen. It was filled with furniture, the size of which Jack had never seen the like before, not even in his bad dreams when he had had the measles. He would have needed a ladder to climb onto the chairs, the cups on the shelves were the size of his mother's mixing bowls, and the gigantic table could have easily housed Margaret and her boy-friend the bull underneath.

Jacked turned incredulously to the little woman who was pulling at his arm. She was still twitching and mewing, but now she was chewing the corner of her grubby apron as well. What a sad, kind, old face, thought Jack. Still sucking her pinny, she panted, "My husband is a cruel giant. He will be home soon, bringing men for supper – not for company, you understand, but to eat. If he hasn't found anybody, he will be in a raging fury. If he finds you, boy, he'll have you for starters. The men down the hall were for a rainy day, but he'll have them for pudding. Heaven know's what I'll make him for his main course . . . my name's Daphne, by the way."

While still nervously munching on her apron and explaining all this, dear old Daphne had served Jack a wonderful meal. He gorged it down gratefully, making deafening slurpings that would have shamed his mother, but not loud enough to drown the sudden sound of a thousand trumpets. Daphne spat out her apron and flung it over her head in fright.

"My husband is here," she squealed from behind the cotton.

"Does he always have trumpets to greet him?" asked Jack, trying not to panic.

"*Trumpets!*" cried Daphne, who was now just a blur, dithering and darting round the kitchen, "that's the beast blowing his nose . . . hide . . . hide."

Jack dived into an open drawer in the towering dresser, and pulled its contents over him for protection. As the monster's footsteps grew louder, the cups on the shelves above him clattered and rattled like the butcher's false teeth. Peering through a chink in his covering, Jack was about to have his first frightening sight of a giant.

The kitchen door crashed open, sending splinters of wood flying through the air like arrows, ricocheting all over the room. Jack could see Daphne cowering under a chair, blinking at the ogre.

"He is enormous," mouthed Jack, trying to take in the terrifying spectacle all at once. The giant's shoes were like two great barges. His legs and arms were not unlike the twisting trunk of the beanstalk. His huge belly hung over his straining trousers, swishing and gurgling from side to side as he stomped around the table. His thick, sweating neck supported a great, bald head that had three stiff hairs on top, which scraped the ceiling making a noise like chalk on a blackboard. His eyes seemed to roll around in opposite directions. He had blue, bulging lips, and a tongue to match, which dangled from one corner of his mouth like a football scarf. It would have made dear Margaret's tongue look like a rose petal.

"Did you have a good day, dear?" mewed Daphne from under the chair.

The ogre kicked the chair away, bellowing "GET UP HAG. I'VE WALKED A MILLION MILES TODAY WITH NOT A HUMAN IN SIGHT. ALL I'VE EATEN SINCE BREAKFAST IS TWO DOPEY DONKEYS. MAKE ME SUPPER, WIFE."

Well, Daphne might have appeared daffy, but she was a wizard in the kitchen. In no time at all, she had set before her husband a positive feast of two roasted sheep, seven steaming loaves and ten wobbling trifles.

"*Bon appetit*, my dear," she whispered.

The giant glowered at the spread. Suddenly he swivelled round in his chair, taking enormous sniffs that made the tablecloth flutter, and boomed, "BLEAT TREAT I SMELL MEN'S MEAT."

"Oh, my dear," shrilled Daphne, sucking her apron again, "it's the men down the hall that you smell."

"BLEEAT TREEAT," the giant bleated back, and he began

sulkily stuffing himself. He started with the trifles first, scooping up the puddings with his fists, slapping them through, and all over, his bulging lips and neck. He soaked up the mess with the seven loaves and finished with the sheep, all in a trice.

"FETCH ME MY GOLDEN HEN, WIFE," he belched.

Daphne disappeared, and after a few seconds scuttled back in carrying a snooty-looking hen, which she placed among the debris on the table.

"LAY, HENNY," burped the beastly giant. To Jack's amusement a glittering, golden egg rolled out from beneath the hen.

"LAY, HENNY," the giant commanded again. The hen screwed up her cocky face and squeezed out golden egg after golden egg. She kept one eye open on her master till he nodded off into a bloated sleep. The hen wearily looked at her evening's work and gave a haughty "PFFF" of disgust at her boss.

Jack did some quick thinking. Losing no time, he leapt silently from the drawer, grabbed the hen, and, before Daphne could swallow her pinny, he dived through the open window and raced for the beanstalk. Jack began his long journey down, down, down to the bottom. There he found his poor, distracted mother exactly where he had left her, praying for her son's return.

"Mum, Mum, I'm back," he panted, holding out to her the golden hen who appeared to have enjoyed the adventure. His mother was beside herself with joy.

"Watch this, Mum. Lay, Henny, lay . . . please?" Miss Hen rewarded Jack with a great pile of golden eggs. Thanking her, Jack scooped up one and sped to the butcher to rescue a jubilant Margaret.

The rest of the golden eggs were a source of income for Jack and Lucy for quite some while, but Jack knew he must keep his promise

to the fairy. So he began to work out a plan to get his revenge on the evil giant.

Knowing Daphne would recognize him, Jack set about disguising himself with a change of clothes and the boot polish trick he had used when younger. Amidst trying to placate his poor, frantic mother, Jack set off up the beanstalk again.

When Jack finally arrived at castle number 49, he knocked once more upon the door, which was opened by Daphne. The poor, demented woman pleaded for him to leave, saying last time she gave shelter to a young boy he had stolen her husband's pet hen. But in the end Jack persuaded her to let him stay.

When the giant returned for his supper, this time Jack hid behind a plant pot stand. After his meal the giant roared for his money bags to be brought before him. His eyes glinted with greed as he started to count Jack's father's gold, kissing each coin before dropping it back into its bag. But, before long, the giant's head lolled forwards, his mouth flopped open, and he began to snore. Without a second thought, Jack again grabbed the bounty, and ran back to the beanstalk as fast as he could.

On his return home, Jack proudly handed over his father's hard-earned money to his mother. This could have kept them in comfort for the rest of their lives, but Jack knew he must make one final journey skywards to prevent the giant from ever repeating his evil deed of years ago.

Jack's mother begged her son to leave well alone, but his new bravery drove him doggedly on – back up the beanstalk. This time his disguise had to be more elaborate than before, or poor old Daphne would become suspicious. So he wrapped himself in white sheeting and arrived at number 49 as an Arab prince.

The little woman again opened the door to his rattlings. She looked an even more sorry sight than before, and her famous apron was now completely chewed in half. Jack's heart began to falter, but he knew he must gain entrance for everyone's sake, and even more for Daphne's. She was almost too weak to mew an argument.

No sooner had Jack got inside the castle, than there came the now familiar mumblings and roarings of 'BLEAT-TREAT-I-SMELL-MEN'S-MEAT.'

The boy watched the giant gorge himself as before, only this time the ogre swilled down his food with crates of wine.

After supper the giant slurred for Daphne to fetch him his golden harp. This was set before him in an instant.

"Play, harp, play," he roared.

"Yes, oh Master," answered the harp, striking up the most delicate harmony. The monster stumbled from his chair and proceeded to dance a ridiculous polka round the kitchen, holding out his shirt like a skirt. He crashed into the dresser, slamming shut the drawer that had been Jack's hide-out and finishing up in a drunken pile with a copper saucepan on his head like a helmet. Luckily, Jack had been one step ahead of him and had leapt out as the giant lumbered towards the dresser, ducking under the ogre's buckling legs.

The harp screamed to her master. As the giant began to stir, Jack grabbed Daphne's bony hand. "Come with me – trust me," he said, willing her to escape with him. He tossed her keys into the prisoners' cage and pulled her away so fast that her feet never touched the dusty ground.

On arriving at the top of the beanstalk, Daphne's squeals of terror were almost as loud as her husband's yelling as he swerved and toppled after them. Jack gave Daphne a piggy-back, and told her not to look down as he descended the beanstalk faster than ever before.

Above them, they could see the giant's feet. As Jack neared the ground, he yelled for his mother to fetch an axe. When he landed, he ordered Lucy to comfort Daphne, and then he began to hack away frantically at the beanstalk. On the final stroke, the tree came crashing down with the giant tangled in its branches . . . he breathed no more.

Jack's mother turned away and the two widows walked slowly into the cosy cottage. The grey fairy appeared beside Jack and gave him a proud wink. With a final wave of her wand, the beanstalk, the giant and the exhausted fairy were gone forever.

In the years following, Lucy and a plump, happy Daphne lived in peace and comfort in neighbouring cottages. Meanwhile, Jack became a hard-working, successful man, as his father had been before him, bringing joy and happiness to everyone.

THE PRINCESS AND THE PEA

As a girl this was always my favourite – and it still is.

THE CHARACTERS

Prince	. . .	*youthful and a little bashful.*
King	. . .	*grand but kindly.*
Queen	. . .	*gentle but firm.*
First Princess	. . .	*a little horsey.*
Second Princess	. . .	*utterly pompous, with a foreign accent.*
Third Princess	. . .	*light voiced and natural.*
Miscellaneous noises	. . .	*neighs, laughs, bird whistles, suppressed laughter.*

There was once a Prince who had reached the stage in life when he longed to marry, but because of the laws of the land his wife had to be a proper Princess. The Prince searched high and low without much success. He even travelled the world to find one, but, although there were many Princesses to see, there was always something not quite right about them. They were either Bad-tempered or Snooty or Vulgar or Unkind or Rude or sometimes even Violent. So in the end he came home and put an advertisement in the greengrocer's window which read:

WANTED

One Princess of exceptional character
Own Bathroom, Crown & Carriage
will be provided
ONLY THE GENUINE NEED APPLY
Ring Palace 1212   Before 10 or after 6

By Thursday, a very excited Prince had had three replies. Appointments were made for each of the three applicants to spend a night at the palace, starting on Monday.

Over the week-end, with the help of the King and Queen, the Prince devised a special plan to find the ideal Princess. They would place a pea (not the green squashy kind, but the dried variety) under the visitor's mattress. If the Princess was soft and gentle, then the pea would give her an uncomfortable night without sleep, and, if she accepted the whole thing with good humour, the Prince had found his perfect bride.

It wasn't really an original plan. The King had used this method very successfully to find the Queen, and he had kept his pea (which was rock hard by now) as a souvenir in his cuff-link box. So, feeling that this particular pea would bring good luck, they carried it proudly to the guest-room and tucked it neatly under the centre of the mattress.

By Monday evening, the Prince was all of a dither with excitement, as the first Princess, dressed very simply in riding gear and wellingtons, came galloping up the drive on a large brown horse. She was a handsome girl with a fine collection of large white teeth. When the Prince suggested they take the horse round the back, the Princess cried, "Oh, push off. Where I go, the horse goes too. It's a case of love me, love my horse." In fact, she insisted it dine with them at the supper table and share her room at night.

In the morning, when the Queen brought the Princess a cup of tea, the room was empty and spotless. The Queen eventually found the Princess grooming and feeding her horse in the *kitchen*!

The Queen inquired whether she had had a good sleep, "Slept like a foal," came the Princess's blunt reply. "Went for a dawn gallop, chopped a stack of logs, and now I must be off to mend my father's carriage. He's all talk, no do. Well you've got my address", and with a brief flash of teeth the Princess galloped off at great speed like a knight charging into battle.

The Prince was somewhat disappointed, not so much in the Princess, whom he admired for her strength and boldness, but because he knew she would tire of his gentle manner.

"All is not lost, son. Let's see what this evening brings," said the Queen, putting an arm round his waist and pulling an understanding face. This always irritated the Prince.

The evening's events were so ghastly that they were almost

funny. A horse and carriage came heaving slowly up the drive, straining and creaking as if it was carrying a ton of wet sand. There was an impatient tugging at the bell, and in swept a sturdy, towering creature with an up-turned nose. She was covered from head to toe in imitation jewelry, and a huge paper crown was balanced on her head. She introduced herself in a superior way with a foreign accent, which was probably imitation too.

Supper was the young Prince's idea of hell. The Princess complained that the food and wine was only fit for peasants, while she gulped and gorged it down with much smacking of lips. She talked nineteen to the dozen, but only of the wonders of hers truly. The Prince and his parents almost choked on the corners of the table-cloth, which they had stuffed in their mouths to stop themselves laughing at the silly girl.

The Princess then started unpinning her hair at the table, and with a great swish of her yellow mane she announced, "I am off to bed. I am booored." She stomped haughtily out of the room, leaving a trail of crumbs and rusty hair pins behind her.

The King, the Queen and the Prince were about to explode with laughter when there came a deafening crack followed by howling from the guest-room. They ran to the room, to find the so-called Princess with her fat legs waving in the air, on a bed which was now just a pile of firewood.

"Try not to look so stupid," she hissed at the Prince. "Order me another bed immediately."

"The shops will be shut at this hour," blurted the Prince.

"Well, tell them who it's for. They'll soon open up for *meeee*," she screamed.

"YOUNG MADAM, you have no right to make such demands, whoever you think you are," shouted the King, who felt like walloping her even though, normally, he was such a quiet man.

The Princess scrambled to her huge feet, and with her mouth as wide open as a railway tunnel shouted back like a spoilt child, "Well . . . anyway . . . when I marry . . . I am going to marry the richest Prince in the whole wide world . . . so there!", and she flounced out. Without waiting for the carriage, she went muttering down the drive, furiously leafing through an atlas and heading for the harbour.

The next morning, there was not much time. The Queen got up early and arrived at the shops just as they were opening. She bought a new bed and twenty mattresses which were going cheap in the sale. She had been so sickened by the night before that she was determined tonight's Princess would have the biggest test of all.

When the new purchases were unwrapped in the guest-room, the Prince helped the Queen to place all twenty mattresses on top of each other on top of the bed. Then the Queen pushed the pea (which luckily hadn't been crushed) underneath the very bottom mattress. "Whoever sleeps in this bed and has an uncomfortable night must be the most soft and sensitive Princess in the whole world, and just right for my son."

"Oh, mother, please don't go on", sighed the bashful Prince, and he went to change before she pulled her 'oh-so-understanding' face.

While the Prince was fixing his disobedient hair and attempting a straight parting, he could hear great claps of thunder and lightning in the distance. The row was getting steadily closer. He drew the curtains on the angry storm and sat down on his bed. "This means the last Princess will be unable to get here", he sighed sadly.

Then, in a silent pause between the thunder claps, there came a short sharp ring on the bell. Standing in the porch silhouetted against the flashing lightning was a very sorry sight. There on the doorstep was a tiny girl with hair hanging down like wet seaweed. Her coat, which had shrunk in the downpour so that it would scarcely fit a baby, revealed skinny little legs in mud-spattered stockings. Her shoes had lost their heels and her mascara was running down her face. She looked like a tiny clown.

"Good evening," she smiled, revealing the brace on her teeth. "I know it's hard to believe looking like this, but I promise I am an absolutely genuine Princess," and she shook her hair like a puppy, so that for a second she stood in a cloud of raindrops. Her hair sprang into a mist of soft dark curls. Flicking a raindrop from the end of her nose, she gave a tinkling laugh and everything glistened – her eyes, her cheeks, her teeth, her brace – but most of all she seemed lit from within.

The Queen rushed her inside and ran a hot bath. She lent the Princess a fluffy, sweet-smelling dressing-gown and slippers, which swamped her. The dining-table was pushed closer to the roaring fire, and the King, Queen and Prince changed into their dressing-gowns and slippers too, so that the Princess would not feel out of place. Over supper they chatted away, swopping stories on this and that. Every now and then, the Prince and Princess would sneak shy glances at each other when they thought no one was looking.

After pudding, the Princess said, "Thank you, that was a delicious meal. I hope I haven't kept you up too late – I can be rather a chatter-box."

"Nonsense, my dear," beamed the King. "You are also a very good listener, and we loved your company. Now, I think we should all get some shut-eye."

The Queen led the Princess to the guest-room, praying their

plan would work. She knew she wouldn't get a wink of sleep herself for fear that the Princess would fail to prove true, although it seemed hardly possible.

The dear Prince was so smitten, he spent the night gazing out of the window waiting for it to get light. He didn't feel tired at all – just anxious.

Dawn brought the most magically beautiful morning, as so often happens after a heavy storm. Eveything looked brand new and vivid, glistening in the sunlight, and the birds sang extra loudly as if to tell the world that the rain had stopped.

The Queen tip-toed along the corridor with a cup of tea for the Princess, closely followed by the King and Prince.

"Darlings," she whispered, "don't come any further. It will seem rude."

So they hid round a corner, but well within earshot.

"Are you awake dear?" called the Queen, tapping gently on the door.

"Oh yes, Ma-am. Please come in."

The Queen, entering the room, peered up to the top of the mattresses at the little Princess. "Did you sleep well?" she inquired nervously.

"Oh, your majesty," replied the Princess, climbing nimbly down, "I hope this doesn't seem ungracious, as it's the cosiest of beds, but, for some reason, I just couldn't get comfy. Perhaps I was too excited, but it is strange that my bottom is all covered in bruises." And she twirled round in her nightie, squealing with laughter. "Look . . . . I look like a currant-bun. Isn't it a hoot."

So the Prince and Princess became engaged, and, after one blissful year of courtship, they were married. And the old, dried-up pea, in a specially-made glass dome, was given pride of place on their bedroom mantelpiece.

THE BOY WHO LEARNT TO SHUDDER

A bit scary!

THE CHARACTERS

Dave	. . .	*a bewildered, but brave and determined lad.*
Clive	. . .	*an academic, but not a brave lad.*
Peter, their father	. . .	*common and downright unpleasant.*
Vicar	. . .	*vicary.*
Vicar's wife	. . .	*almost too sweet for words.*
Hiker	. . .	*hearty and quite poshly spoken.*
Landlady	. . .	*jovial and rural.*
Panthers	. . .	*menacingly breathy.*
Half-a-man	. . .	*goblinish.*
White spirit	. . .	*fierce despite his age.*
King	. . .	*Prince Charles-ish.*
Princess	. . .	*Princess Diana-ish.*
Miscellaneous noises	. . .	*cheers, heavy breathing, chuckles, cackles, mews, giggles.*

Once there was a man called Peter who had two sons. The oldest boy, called Clive, was a naturally clever student. The younger of the two, Dave, didn't have that sort of mind, but he was strong and brave. Dave longed to be like his older brother, if only to please his father who cruelly favoured Clive and had no interest in his youngest son. Dave was never encouraged or praised, was never read to or spoken to. In fact he was virtually ignored, so his poor brain hardly stood a chance and it became very sluggish indeed.

When the father needed any errands run, he only ever called for "Clever Clive", adding spitefully, "It's no good asking 'Dippy Dave', he's bound to bungle it." So poor Dave came to believe he would.

If on these errands Clive had to pass the garden with the angry Alsatian, or cut through the churchyard, or other such spooky places, he would arrive home very green around the gills panting, "How I'm shuddering."

Dave, seeing his brother being praised as if he'd been to the moon and back and given a chocolate bar as a reward, would whisper longingly, "If only I could learn to shudder . . ."

"Father," he eventually had the nerve to utter one day, "I am sorry that I trouble you so, but if you haven't the time to teach me anything else, *please* could you teach me to shudder?"

Peter shouted in the poor boy's face, "You'll put me in an early grave with all your daffy questions. Get out of my sight."

So Dave hid in the garden shed and tapped out his frustrations on a row of plant pots, chanting, "I-will-learn-to-shudder-I-will-learn-to-shudder . . ."

That evening the local vicar was doing his rounds, and over a glass or two of sherry Peter bleated on and on about "The Youth of Today", moaning and lying through his teeth that after *all* his love and care, *all* his youngest son wanted to do in life was to learn to shudder. "He'll be the death of me, vicar," he said.

The vicar, being very holy, believed that Peter had had his work cut out for him bringing up Dave, so downing his sherry he said, "Let Dave stay with my wife and me for a few days. I'll soon teach him how to shudder."

Peter was only too happy to be rid of his duties to his son and packed Dave off in a rush.

During the following week, the vicar and his wife (who had children of their own) thoroughly enjoyed Dave's amusing company. With a little effort and encouragement he was coming along in leaps and bounds, learning to read and write, do up his laces and buttons, eat quietly, and generally realizing that he wasn't so useless after all – except he still hadn't learnt how to shudder. So the vicar, who had grown to love the boy, decided he must keep his promise to the neglectful father.

"Dave," he said, "tonight I would like you to ring the bells for me. I know you will do it very well."

"If you think I can, then I know I can," Dave proudly replied.

So that evening Dave swang on the ropes in the belfry with all his might, causing the hefty bells to ring and chime as if they were in St Paul's Cathedral. Dave imagined he was playing for a royal wedding, with the Queen Mother and the crowds cheering up at him. Just as he was about to step out onto the balcony of the palace with the newly-weds, his dream was broken by a vision of floating white lurking silently in the shadows.

"Who do you think you are and what on earth are you dressed as?" shouted Dave, carrying on with his good work.

The ghostly figure said nothing, but it started wailing and walking towards him.

The boy gave a final tug on the ropes, saying, "Look, you can't frighten me. My gym mistress is more scary looking than you." He gave the ghost a gentle shove, making it topple down the stone steps. "I did warn you", said Dave, as he scampered past the ghost.

Dave ran into the house and scrambled into bed, hoping to continue his royal dream, but all he managed was one about his father, greedily munching a million chocolate bars, ordering a starving Dave to sweep away the wrappers which were fluttering all around and away from him.

He was woken by the vicar's wife calling, "Dave, oh Dave, have you seen my husband? He didn't return after evensong."

"All I saw was a ghost trying to haunt me, so I shoved him down the stairs," answered the boy, who was now very concerned too.

"That was my beloved husband," gasped the sweet woman. "He was trying to give you your longed-for lesson in shuddering."

The two ran up to the belfry. There they found the poor vicar nursing a broken ankle. "It was a very silly way to try to scare you, dear boy," he said. "You were magnificent in the way you handled it. Now don't you reproach yourself for anything. You are a smashing little lad and never forget that. I got everything I deserved for playing such a daft prank."

But despite the vicar's kind words, the poor boy still felt an utter nuisance, and he said he had better go home before he caused any more trouble.

Several uneventful years later, Peter felt he could at last lawfully kick his youngest son out into the world, which was something he would have liked to have done as soon as the poor boy taught himself to walk. One day he said to Dave, "Look son, you look sturdy enough now to go and find work and keep yourself, though goodness knows what you'll do. Here are a few coins. Don't tell anyone where you came from, or who your father is, for I am ashamed of you."

The young lad took the coins, and said, "I'll do my best Father. I'll even learn to shudder," just before the door was slammed and bolted in his face.

Dave pocketed the coins sadly, took a deep breath, and set off on the next stage of his young life, muttering "I will learn to shudder," for miles and miles.

A hiker with a big red face was stomping along stoutly behind him carrying an enormous knapsack with clattering saucepans and tin mugs dangling from it, and even he could hear him muttering. He puffed alongside Dave and shouted above the rattlings, "NICE DAY FOR A RAMBLE. WHAT'S YOUR NAME?"

"I don't know," answered Dave.

"WHAT'S YOUR FATHER'S NAME THEN?"

"I can't tell you."

"WELL WHAT ON EARTH DO YOU KEEP MUTTER-ING? YOU'VE BEEN DOING IT FOR MILES!"

"That I must learn to shudder."

"NOW LOOK HERE, OLD BOY," said the traveller, swishing away the brambles with a stick, "THIS COUNTRY AIR AND TOO MUCH WALKING IS MAKING YOU LIGHT-HEADED. THERE'S A GOOD 'BED AND BREAKFAST' AFTER THE NEXT FIELD WHERE YOU CAN REST UP FOR THE NIGHT. THEN IF YOU CARE TO DISCUSS YOUR PLANS WITH ME IN THE MORNING, I WILL BE HAPPY TO TRY AND HELP."

The young boy was grateful for the hiker's kind advice, as his boots were steaming and his young legs were buckling with fatigue.

The next morning the breakfast room of the "Bed and Breakfast" was crowded with other travellers wearing whiskery socks and bulging knapsacks, eating noisily whilst consulting their maps.

Dave sat down by his kindly red-faced friend and repeated his sad tale. The landlady, whose sole aim in life was to make everyone happy, overheard their conversation. "Now son," she interrupted, for she treated everyone like a relation, "I know the very place you can learn to shudder. In the next village is an enchanted castle. If any young man can manage to stay there for three nights, the King has promised his daughter's hand in marriage, for in the castle are treasures guarded by evil spirits. That treasure would then be shared with you, making a poor boy very rich indeed. Many have gone to the castle and never returned, but I sense you are a very brave boy who deserves a life of good fortune."

The youth thanked the jolly woman and his friend for their help, and with hearty well-wishes and a flurry of maps from the breakfast-room, he was sent on his way with confidence.

That afternoon Dave asked the King if he may be permitted to watch for three nights in the enchanted castle.

The King looked him over and liked what he saw. "You may indeed," he said. "You may also ask for three things to take with you into the castle, but they must be lifeless things mind."

Dave thought for a while, then answered in a very adult voice, "I should like a fire, a carpenter's bench, and a lathe with the knife that belongs to it."

The King said, "That sounds like a sensible list", and ordered the three items to be delivered to the castle.

At the castle as night was starting, Dave made a bright fire. He put the carpenter's bench and the lathe and the knife beside it, and, crouching down beside them, he began to dream. "If only I could shudder," he thought yet again, "but I won't learn how to here."

His thoughts were disturbed by a loud mewing sound coming from one corner of the dark room. "Mew, we're freezing!"

"Then come and sit by the fire, nitwits, and warm yourselves," Dave answered.

Two enormous black panthers bounded out and in one leap they landed beside him, staring with wild red eyes.

"Let's play cards," they breathed in his face.

"Sure," said the boy, "but let's see your paws first."

They waved their glinting claws at him.

"My goodness your nails need a trim," he said quickly grabbing hold of the panthers by the scruff of their necks. He dumped them on the bench, screwed their paws into the lathe, and pulled out their claws with the knife. Then he tossed the two cats into the moat down below. But no sooner had he silenced those two, and was returning to his seat by the fire, than from every hole and corner in the room came hordes of screaming wild black cats and dogs dragging red hot chains that whipped and lashed around them. They scratched and spat at the fire with their foaming jaws.

Dave watched them calmly for a while. Then, when he decided the time was ripe, he jumped onto the carpenter's bench brandishing the knife over his head, shouting wildly. Some animals leapt cowardly through the windows and were drowned. Those that leapt at the boy were flung into the moat too.

Finally Dave stood exhausted, but alone, over the remainder of his fire. He looked round for somewhere to sleep, and seeing a huge iron bed at the far end of the room, he laid down gratefully.

Just as sleep was beginning to sweep over him he felt the bed start to move. It began to lumber on stiff legs through the castle.

Dave shouted out, "That's right, go as fast as you like," as it trotted up and down the stone stairways. All at once, it turned topsy-turvy and landed on top of him like a mountain. He flung away the mattress and pillows, calling, "Whoever chooses can have a ride now," and he lay down by the fire and slept soundly.

In the morning the King came in and seeing him lying there thought he was dead. "What a pity, he was a brave lad – a fine match for my girl," he said sadly.

The boy heard this and leapt to his feet. The King, much relieved, asked him what sort of night he had had.

"Oh fine," answered Dave.

On the second night, Dave again sat by the fire in the castle and began his old song, "I wish I could sh . . ." when he heard a terrible scrambling and scraping in the chimney. After a pause, out jumped half a man with a cruel face who landed beside him.

"Half-a-mo," said the half-a-man, "the other half will be down in half-a-tick," and sure enough the remainder clattered down.

"Let me stoke up the fire," said Dave, not knowing which way to look.

When he turned round again the two halves were joined together, but back to front. It really was a gruesome sight.

The muddle of a man started prodding the boy away from the fire with grubby fingers. Then again there were loud scramblings in the chimney, and out poured more men even more hideous than the first. Some had legs where arms should be, some with bodies or heads back to front. One was even upside down with his head between his legs, while his arms waved in the air. Between them they carried nine bones and two skulls. Ignoring Dave, they set these up for a game of skittles.

"Can I play?" called the boy.

"If you have money," they cackled.

"Oh, I've money enough. But wait, your bowls are not round," and so saying he gave the skulls a turn in the lathe.

"So," he cried, "they'll bowl much better now."

Dave lost a little money, but no matter. When the clock struck

twelve, everything disappeared from sight, and he lay down quietly and went to sleep.

When the third night came, Dave sat down on the bench and said crossly, "If only I could shud . . ."

Suddenly the tallest man that Dave had ever seen entered the room. He was oldish, hideous too, with long wispy white hair and beard, and he carried an oversize axe. "Oh you wretch," he cried. "Now you shall shudder, for you are going to die."

"Hang on just a minute," said Dave. "If I am to die, let me think about it first."

"I'LL SOON MAKE AN END OF YOU," the apparition roared back.

"Softly, softly," whispered the youth. "Don't be so big-headed. I think I am as strong as you, perhaps even stronger."

"WELL IF YOU ARE, I SHALL LET YOU GO," and the old man cut the bench in half with one swipe of the axe.

"I can do better than that," boasted Dave, and with a flick of his knife he drove it into the bench, wedging the old man's beard tightly down with it. "Now I have caught you and it's your turn to die."

The old man whimpered and pleaded with the boy to release him, promising him great riches. So Dave withdrew the knife.

The tall man led him down dark corridors leading to a room containing three crates of gold. "One is for the poor," he said, "one is for the King, and the third is for you."

The clock struck twelve and the spirit disappeared, leaving Dave standing alone in the dark. "I must get back," he thought, and he groped his way to his room and fell asleep in front of the fire.

Next morning the King came again, calling, "Well, I bet this time you learnt what it is to shudder."

"Not at all," Dave replied. "An old man came and showed me a great deal of gold, but he didn't mention shuddering."

"Well, you have disenchanted the castle," said the King, "and you shall marry my sweet daughter."

"That's all very nice, but I don't know yet how to sh . . .", but the King had already left to fetch the boy's share of gold and to organize the wedding celebrations.

Dave was a marvellous husband and he loved his little wife to pieces, but she confessed to the jolly landlady over a mug of tea at the "Bed and Breakfast" that it did worry her when the Prince kept muttering "I can't shudder" in his sleep.

"Oh, is he *still* going on about that? We'll have to stop him once and for all."

So they worked out a plan. They filled a bucket with icy water and goldfish from the stream. Then they carried it up to the palace where the Prince was having forty winks in a deck-chair in the garden. They crept up to him and upturned the bucket over his head, spilling the water and flopping fish all over him.

"Uh-uh", cried Dave with a start and his teeth began to chatter, "I-I-I am shud-d-d-ering . . . YOU'VE M-MADE M-ME SH-SH-SHUDDER."

The little Princess, the landlady and Dave did roly-poly's all round the lawn hooting with laughter, for his stupid quest had been fulfilled. When they landed in a happy heap in the duck pond they laughed even more, saying perhaps it wasn't so stupid after all, as without it the three of them would never have met.

"Oh Dad, if you could see me now!" spluttered Prince Dave, straightening his crown, and the happy threesome ran laughing and shuddering into the palace to find some dry clothes and to put the kettle on.

THE EMPEROR'S NEW CLOTHES

Or the King's come-down.

THE CHARACTERS

Emperor	. . .	*a vain, foppish dandy.*
Brothers	. . .	*slimy.*
Detective	. . .	*Bob Hoskins, of course.*
Butler	. . .	*standard, all-purpose butler voice.*
Officials	. . .	*vicar-like.*
Child	. . .	*voice of innocence.*
Mother	. . .	*embarrassed.*
Miscellaneous noises	. . .	*cheers, gasps, stifled giggles, hoots of laughter.*

Hundreds of years ago, there was an Emperor who couldn't think of anything but clothes. He hardly cared about his country at all – all he did care about was showing off his latest outfit. When he dined with friends, he would leave the table after one course and return in a different outfit for the next. Playing tennis with him was a nightmare. Each time he'd hit a ball, he'd scuttle from the court and reappear in an even more elaborate tennis get-up. If he visited the theatre, he caused havoc. He'd rush from the Royal Box to change after each scene, leaving the poor actors and the audience to talk amongst themselves until he was reseated. With an exhausted orchestra striking up 'God Save the King' on each re-entry, no one could remember what the play was about!

In other countries people said, "the King is in office"; here they said, "the King is in wardrobe". He had as many wardrobes as jackets: the top three floors of the palace were completely given over to them, where they stood row upon row like an overcrowded housing estate.

Now, two crafty brothers, who had heard about the Emperor's obsession, journeyed to the city with the intention of tricking the fool into giving them his money. These brothers were very weird, not so much because they looked identical, but because they moved and spoke at the same time as if they shared one brain.

The crafty pair, knowing that news travels fast, swaggered about the city proclaiming that they were "master weavers and tailors, skilled to perfection in Paris", boasting that they could "weave the most wonderful cloth imaginable, never before seen in this unfashionable country", and claiming that "the cloth has such unique patterns and colours, there is none like it in the whole world". Besides this, they lied, "the material has a secret ingredient which means that only clever people will be able to see it".

Sure enough, the Emperor soon heard of this, and he summoned the strange pair for a meeting. The two brothers told their pack of lies, using jerky gestures and identical speeches in unison, and the Emperor listened intently, while darting in and out of wardrobes, appearing and reappearing each time in different get-ups.

"This indeed would be a valuable cloth," thought the Emperor, taking a much-needed breather. Already, he could see himself dressed in the best clothes in the whole world, admired by all who saw him. "Yes, I must have some woven for me at once and made up into a new suit of clothes," and he paid the two rogues a pile of money in advance to steam ahead.

So, the brothers set up two looms and pretended to weave away, but of course the looms had nothing on them. They demanded the finest silk and pure gold thread, which they carefully hid away, and then they carried on weaving well into the night on empty looms, knowing full well that their shadows would be seen by the whole city.

Everyone was talking about "this new-fangled cloth" that the two rascals had also claimed "only the brainy could see", and they were all dying to find out which of their neighbours were thick.

So indeed was the Emperor. He thought *he* had no worries on *that* score, but he decided it was safer to send someone else to see for the first time. "I will send my private detective; he's a clever man who can best detect what the cloth is like."

The two impostors were frantically working the looms when the detective entered carrying an enormous magnifying glass. "HMMM," he thought. "Well, I'm blowed if I can see nuffink, but can't let on or 'is 'ighness will fink I'm barmy, and unfit for the job . . . HO, HO, nice bit of cloff you've got there," he lied badly.

"Come close", they called in unison, "to fully appreciate the beauty of the colours and patterns. Look at this brilliant zig-zag effect."

"YUS, YUS," he said, staring at nothing, "I like the stripes an' all."

"SPOTS", they snapped back like two old women.

The detective gave a hurried excuse and left before he gave more false evidence. Once outside, he hastily filled up his notebook with as many clues as he could remember.

The two brothers sent two identical letters in one envelope demanding more money, silk and golden thread. When this was received, they stashed it away in a locked trunk and continued to clatter away on their empty looms.

After his detective's detailed report, the Emperor could hardly contain his curiosity, but he decided that one more trusted servant should view the cloth before him.

This time he sent his old, faithful butler – a man who loved his job, but who feared that it would soon be taken over by a much younger man. The butler creaked up the stairs to the workroom door and rang the bell. When it was opened by the twins, he announced stiffly, "YOU RANG, SIRS."

"No, you did, you silly old fool," they answered together, smirking at each other and handing him their hats. "I suppose you've been sent to inspect HIS LORDSHIP'S cloth before SUPPER IS SERVED," they chanted sarcastically.

"YES, SIRS," the poor old man replied, for he was used to turning a blind eye to bad manners.

So the brothers jumped to their looms, and pretended to weave at a demented rate. "What do you see, JEEVES?"

"Oh . . . oh . . . it's beautiful," the butler answered sadly, convinced that his senses had finally left him and that he should hand in his notice. "I . . . I wish I had worn my stronger glasses to see it even better." Then, remembering the detective's report, he blurted out quickly, "But I can see fine zig-zags and spots. WILL THAT BE ALL, SIRS?"

"CHECKS AND SPECKS", they shrieked, forgetting their own first description.

The old man shuffled in confusion to the door, saying, "THIS WAY, SIR", as he led himself down the stairs.

Later, he told the Emperor, "It's magnificent M'LORD, um . . . all . . . stars and . . . dots . . .", hoping that his poor old memory was still working.

By now the whole town was buzzing with excitement, for the Emperor was at last to view the final work together with two officials from his court.

"Ah, your Majesty, our work is almost complete, come see for your royal selves," smarmed the crafty brothers, bowing so low that their hair swept the floor.

The Emperor and his officials stood blinking at the empty loom. "Oh help," thought the King. "Does this mean I am unfit to be Emperor? That would be the end of my world if it were true."

The two officials were also doubting their own sanity, but they nodded fast, cooing and gurgling at the empty looms. "Your Majesty," spoke one of the officials, wiping his brow. "It is SO spectacular; you must have it made up into a suit of clothes to wear at tomorrow's procession."

This news soon spread through the city and people started to camp in the streets to be sure of a good view.

That evening, the brothers lit many candles in the workshop to be sure their shadows could be seen making the Emperor's new suit of clothes. They pulled great lengths of pretend cloth from empty

looms, snipping the air with giant scissors and sewing with empty needles.

"Finished at last," they declared at dawn, shaking hands in an exaggerated way. Then, folding up nothingness and packing it up carefully, they sauntered snootily past an admiring crowd, carrying boxes with "By Appointment to the Royals" scribbled on the side.

The Emperor rushed them into his royal boudoir and hovered over the odd couple who, with great economy, slowly started to open the boxes.

"Close your eyes, Your Worshipness," they demanded. "Now open . . . VOILA!" and they stood side by side with their arms in the air, holding nothing. "Are not these clothes exquisite? We have brought Paris to your doorstep."

The King gulped and blinked, nodding slowly, while they rushed around him crying, "See the cut of the jacket, the softness of the cloak," as they pretended to hold garments against him.

The Emperor, trying not to look daft, gradually started to believe the whole pantomime. "Now, you must help me change," he spluttered, flinging off all his clothes. He posed in front of the mirror, while the brothers mimed dressing him in a baggy hat, hose and jacket. They smoothed out creases and did up buttons which tickled but didn't exist. Then, with the flourish of a bullfighter, they draped him in an imaginary cloak, and snapped their fingers at two page boys whose duty it was to carry the end corners of the long cloak. The two lads thought they were in a madhouse as they were forced to grapple with unseen corners at the far end of the room, scraping their knuckles on the ground as they made fists to yank up the invisible robe. They followed their naked master out into the sunlight, past the gasping crowds.

The Emperor pompously led the procession, giving lordly waves to his admirers, who, after their initial shock, quickly remembered to look brainy and began to cheer the ridiculous spectacle. Then, all of a sudden, loud and clear above the cheers of the crowd, a child's voice was heard: "Mum, why isn't the Emperor wearing his clothes? I can see all his rude bits."

The boy's poor mother laughed nervously, and shouted to the crowd, "Listen to the voice of innocence; *he* said the Emperor is wearing no clothes."

Soon everyone was whispering the same thing, getting louder and louder: "THE EMPEROR IS WEARING NO CLOTHES."

The poor King covered his important bits and, beginning to shiver and shake, started to believe the child himself. Then, remembering who he was, he pulled his haughtiest face and majestically continued his march. He was, however, oblivious to the state of the procession behind him, for all were bent double with laughter. The soldiers, the officials, the pageboys *and* the horses, were all pointing to the crowd to look at the Emperor's you-know-what.

HANSEL AND GRETHEL

A story of neglect and ill-treatment that ends in true happiness.

THE CHARACTERS

Hansel	. . .	*a strong, wise boy.*
Grethel	. . .	*a strong, wise girl.*
Mother	. . .	*a drawling, cunning voice.*
Father	. . .	*Bob Hoskins, of course.*
Witch	. . .	*old and evil.*
King	. . .	*down to earth and basically nice.*

A woodcutter and his wife lived in a remote cottage at the edge of a forest, with their son and daughter, Hansel and Grethel. Now this couple should never have had children, for they were basically selfish people, and, although having babies had seemed a nice idea, they did not realize that being parents would be such hard work – until it was too late. They treated their children very badly. They never played with them or talked to them; they never read to them, or gave them toys; and they never kissed, tickled or cuddled them. Instead, they beat them or screamed at them; but, more often than not, they just ignored them, sometimes for weeks on end. As their home was so far away from the nearest village, Hansel and Grethel never played with other children, and so they grew up believing that this was the way that all parents treated their children.

Yet, despite this neglect, Hansel and Grethel were good and kind, and they tried so hard to please their mother and father. They would get up very early to do all the chores while their lazy parents slept, and they'd work without resting all day long. After a simple supper of water and boiled potatoes, they would silently clear up after themselves, and then creep to their cold, dark room to play with their "treasure trunk". This was a battered box full of their "toys". Inside was a jar containing acorns which they used for playing marbles, ten pine cones for a game of skittles, a doll Grethel had made from twigs and rags, a set of soldiers Hansel had made from bottle corks, and an old, rusty tin full of tiny pieces of broken, coloured glass which they had collected over the years and which they had polished like jewels with a smooth pebble and a bit of spit.

As Hansel and Grethel were quietly playing one evening, they overheard their mother and father talking in the room below.

"My love," their mother said, "if we didn't have any kids, we would have *so* much more of *everything* for ourselves. If we got *rid* of them, just think beloved, we could stay in bed all day, have double portions of food for our supper, and just come and go as we please without a care in the world. We could even let their room to a couple of lodgers – why we could be *so* rich."

Hansel's and Grethel's hearts were thumping as they heard their father reply, "I know my love – but what do you mean by 'get rid of them'?"

"Well, first thing tomorrow morning, we could all go for a long walk into the forest and sort of . . . lose them."

"Yes dear . . . but there are wild animals deep in the forest of a night time."

"Exactly, my dear!"

Hansel and Grethel held each other tightly. "Don't worry," Hansel whispered. "I have a plan . . ."

Much later, when their parents were sleeping soundly, Hansel and Grethel crept downstairs. They collected a pile of small, white pebbles from the garden, packing them deep into Hansel's jacket pockets, and returned silently to their room to sleep.

In the morning Hansel and Grethel were woken by their parents standing over them, calling, "Wake up, little treasures. It's such a beautiful day that we thought we'd go on a family outing. We haven't done that for a while, have we?"

"We've never done it," thought Hansel.

That morning the children ate a huge breakfast, and for the first time in their lives their stomachs felt full. Just before they were all ready to leave, their mother even gave them some bread in case they got peckish on the journey. Grethel quickly offered to carry both portions in her tattered apron, as she knew Hansel's pockets were full of pebbles.

So the family began their walk. Once they entered an unfamiliar area of the forest, Hansel lagged slightly behind the others, carefully dropping a white pebble every yard or so. "OH, DO KEEP UP WITH US, BOY" shouted his father, but remembering just in time that he was supposed to be nice to the children, he added sweetly, "We don't want to lose you now, do we?"

When it began to get dark their father said to them, "Now my little darlings, you rest here for a moment while your mother and I go to find some blackberries. Then we'll all set off home for a fish and chips tea." And, without even a backward glance, the heartless parents disappeared into the bushes and were gone.

Hansel sat beside Grethel on the soft grass and told her his plan. "We will eat our bread slowly and drink fresh water from the stream. We'll find two small rocks to bang together every now and then to scare away wild animals, and then, as soon as it's dark, we'll start on our journey home."

"Why must we wait until it's dark?" trembled Grethel.

"You'll see," he smiled bravely, hoping she couldn't hear his knees knocking.

When night fell, it was as if they had crawled into a black velvet tent with their eyes shut. Suddenly a brilliant moon appeared in the sky as if a light had been switched on.

"This is why we waited until dark, Grethel. Look behind you." There, disappearing into the darkness was a winding trail of white pebbles glistening in the moonlight. "Let's go."

So they journeyed bravely home following the pebble trail, banging the two rocks together (the fierce anti-animal device).

When at last they reached the cottage, the noise from within was a deafening mixture of peals of laughter and raucous singing. Hansel and Grethel rang the bell loudly several times.

As the door was opened the expression on their parents' faces was pathetically ridiculous. Their eyes jiggled in their sockets, whilst their mouths zipped and unzipped grotesque grins. "Where on earth did you two disappear to?" they managed to splutter. "We have been *out of our minds with worry* . . . now get to bed before we belt you."

Poor Hansel and Grethel staggered into their room and collapsed onto the sacks in an exhausted sleeping heap.

Two nights later, the children again heard their mother and father planning to be rid of them. When everyone was asleep, they again crept downstairs to find some more pebbles, but this time the door was tightly locked and the key hidden.

In the morning, as the four set off into the forest, Hansel pocketed the bread that his mother gave him and left a trail of white crumbs as he had done before with the pebbles.

When they reached the thickest part of the forest, their parents made some excuse and disappeared into the undergrowth.

Hansel and Grethel waited patiently for nightfall, but this evening the moon only lit up a mass of forest.

"Oh Hansel!" Grethel cried, "the birds must have eaten the crumbs."

"Come on Grethel, it's not like you to go all soggy on me, we must be brave. We'll make a bed under these dried leaves and take it in turns to sleep. I am sure everything will be all right."

In the morning Hansel and Grethel collected blackberries and pine nuts for breakfast. They ate so much that they got hiccups, and their faces and hands were crimson from the berry juice. They fell about in a fit of the giggles, partly at the state of each other, and partly because they were so relieved to be still alive. Then they scrubbed themselves clean in the stream and almost drank it dry.

When they were quite ready, the two set off for "home". But sad

to say, after many weary hours of walking they were hopelessly lost. "Let's just try this small path here," said Grethel.

After a while they could see ahead of them a strange house no bigger than a garden shed. It was made not from bricks or wood, but from sweets! The windows were large wine-gums and the walls were pebbled with millions of smarties. The door was a solid slab of toffee, the chimney was a giant bar of chocolate, and the roof was tiled with flat mints. Hansel and Grethel eagerly began to break off bits of the sweets to feed their painful hunger.

Suddenly a voice from inside the house called "Nibble, nibble, who's nibbling my house?"

Hansel and Grethel froze in mid-chew as they watched the toffee-door creak open. Out tottered a tiny old woman, bent double with age, and her head shaking from side to side as if she was continually saying "no".

"Dear little children," she croaked, "you look half starved and exhausted. Do come inside and get some proper food down you and have a good rest. No harm will come to you here." She took them by the hand and led them into the house.

Inside, a hot supper was waiting for them – hamburgers, followed by pancakes with syrup and a blob of cream. Afterwards, two little white beds were uncovered, and Hansel and Grethel lay down in them and fell into a deep, peaceful sleep.

But the old woman was only pretending to be friendly. She was really a wicked old witch who lay in wait for children, and she had built her house of sweets to lure them to her. When she had caught them, she would fatten them up and eat them. Although she had tiny red eyes that could hardly see, her nose was like an animal's and she could smell the flesh of human children for miles around. She watched over Hansel and Grethel as they slept and seeing their rosy cheeks muttered to herself, "What a nice juicy pair they'll be. I'll have them on toast with a dollop of tomato sauce."

In the morning the witch dragged Hansel from his sleep with her strong, scrawny hands and flung him into a small cage outside. She pressed her pleated mouth through the bars, and shouted into Hansel's sleepy face, "I'm going to eat you . . . when I've fattened you up."

Then she grabbed Grethel from her bed and screamed at her, "Get up and make some food for your brother, because as soon as he is plump I shall eat him, and then I shall do the same to you."

Poor Grethel was forced to take her brother some food. She desperately tried to unlock his cage, but she was flung aside by the old hag.

Next morning the witch went to Hansel's cage and shouted, "Boy, stick out a finger so I can test how plump you are getting."

Hansel stuck a small chicken bone through the bars of the cage, but, as the old witch was almost blind, she couldn't tell the difference. She felt the thin bone and shouted in disgust, "Not fat enough", and hobbled indoors.

This happened every day, until one morning the witch shook Grethel awake, saying, "I can wait no longer. Tomorrow I shall eat your brother for breakfast and you for tea."

Grethel pretended to cry bitterly, but as soon as the witch was out of sight, she ran to her brother. "Quickly, Hansel, we must find a way to escape. We are both to be eaten tomorrow," she whispered.

"I thought as much," her dear brother replied. "I have managed to loosen the lock. While I escape, you must grab the witch's magic wand and whistle from above the fireplace . . . only quickly Grethel."

Grethel fetched the wand and whistle, and away the children ran as fast as their legs could carry them.

But before very long the wicked witch discovered they had gone. She put on her large, yellow, magic boots which went yards at a step, and she had hardly taken more than a few steps before she overtook them.

In a flash Grethel waved the magic wand and turned her brother into a lake and herself into a swan swimming in the middle of it. The old witch tried to entice her to the shore with cake crumbs, but after many hours she had to hobble off in a huff without her prisoners.

With the help of the wand, Grethel changed them both back to normal. They began to escape once more, running through the night. As day broke, they knew it would not be long before the witch came clattering after them again in her big yellow boots. So Grethel turned herself into a rose on a thorn bush, which Hansel sat beside playing a tune on the magic whistle.

Sure enough old yellow boots *did* appear, saying, "My, what a fine musician you are young man. You should be famous if you are not already. Please carry on playing while I pick some roses." But the whistle was magic and forced whoever came near the player to dance like someone demented. The old lady's legs and arms flew in all directions until at last they were all tied up in a big reef-knot. Hansel set Grethel free with the wand and they escaped yet again.

After many hours, Hansel and Grethel had to rest. They scrambled under a pile of leaves and fell into a sound sleep.

As they slept, the witch – who had managed to untangle her knotted limbs – stood over them. She snatched up her wand and whistle and changed Hansel into a fawn before disappearing.

In the morning when Grethel awoke and discovered what had happened to her brother, she threw her tiny arms round his neck and, as tears poured down her face, said, "I will never leave your side Hansel. I will look after you always and you will never come to harm."

Together, Hansel and Grethel built a home beside the stream from woven branches and twigs, backed with mud and grit. They lined the floor of their house with a carpet of dried grass. Every morning Grethel picked berries and nuts for herself and juicy leaves and grass for her fawn. At night, she curled up beside him and fell asleep with her head on his side. If only Hansel had been his true form they could have had such a happy life at last.

After many years had passed and Grethel had grown into a beautiful young woman, it happened that one day the King came hunting in the forest. When the fawn heard the trumpets and the excited hounds, he pleaded with Grethel to let him join the chase. "I can no longer be so protected. I must take my chances outside and use all my energy and strength."

The fawn begged so long that she at last let him go. "But please be home by evening. If you call 'Sister, let me in', I shall know it is you and let you in."

Hansel gave his sister a gentle butt. Then he bounded out into the forest teasing the hounds to give chase. The King spotted his unusual grace and ordered his huntsmen after him, but Hansel's power was so great that he out-galloped the team. When it grew dark, the fawn returned home and called, "Sister, let me in".

Next morning the hunt continued and on hearing the huntsman's horn, the fawn again pleaded, "Sister let me go."

As soon as the King saw the beautiful fawn, he again ordered his huntsmen to give chase. The hunt lasted all day, but at last the huntsmen surrounded the fawn and wounded one of his legs. Hansel limped slowly home not knowing he was being followed by the hunter who had hurt him. When he saw the animal call "Sister, let me in" at the door of the cottage, and the door opening and shutting again, he raced back to tell the King.

Grethel was distressed to see her brother so badly wounded, but she bathed his leg clean and bound it with healing herbs.

In the morning there was not a sign of the wound, and on hearing the hunt start again, the little fawn begged to go once more.

"No, I am sure they will kill you this time. I can't let you go."

"Please, sister, I mustn't give up now," and so he was gone, galloping through the forest for all to see.

"There he goes," shouted the King, "chase him until he is caught, but no one hurt him."

So the chase went on until sunset, but Hansel outstripped everyone and at last went home with pride to his relieved sister.

"Right, show me this hut," said the King to the hunter who had wounded the fawn.

When they reached the door, the King called "Sister, let me in".

In her confusion Grethel opened the door.

"May I come in?" asked the King, removing his crown. "This hunting is thirsty work. I don't suppose you have the kettle on by any chance, do you?"

"Of course," she replied, forgetting to curtsey.

The King had never met such an interesting girl, who could look after herself so well, living happily with her fawn. He found excuses to visit her every day.

After a few months the couple had fallen in love, and the King asked Grethel to marry him. She replied that she could not marry until a way was found for the fawn to be turned back into her brother. "YOUR BROTHER", laughed the King, flabbergasted, for Grethel had never told him the story of the witch for fear he would think her dotty. But now she told him everything.

"Oh that wretched witch. I know her well," said the King, and he ordered his men to find her.

When the witch was brought before him, the King ordered her to release poor Hansel from his spell, and so the joyful brother and sister were reunited.

Grethel married her kind King and Hansel became his royal counsellor. The King's wedding gift to Grethel was a silver box full of diamonds, rubies and emeralds which was inscribed on the lid: "These won't need a pebble and spit!" I hope their wicked parents got to hear about it. Their faces would be a picture.